BUMPED
AND
THUMPED

BY IAN TREVASKIS

ILLUSTRATED BY CRAIG SMITH

HOUGHTON MIFFLIN COMPANY
BOSTON
ATLANTA DALLAS GENEVA, ILLINOIS PALO ALTO PRINCETON

Grownups are so mean!
They don't realize what some
kids go through. Why, I'm lucky
to still be alive and in one piece.

✚

I've been bumped and thumped,
walloped and whacked,
pummelled and pounded,
crunched and clobbered. But do
you think they care? No way!

✚

Every time I'm about to collapse
from loss of blood, or have
broken every bone in my body,
they say the same thing . . .

"Just give it a rub,"
says Mom.

"Go and lie down for
a while," says Dad.

"Come here and I'll kiss
it better," says Grandma.

When I'm surfing the Pipeline at Waikiki and
I'm wiped out by an awesome wave and my
whole body has been mashed and mangled,
what do they say?

"Just give it a rub,"
says Mom.

"Go and lie down for
a while," says Dad.

"Come here and I'll kiss
it better," says Grandma.

When I tumble out of the crow's-nest of my
pirate ship and crash to the heaving deck in
the middle of a fierce storm and I'm bruised
and battered all over, what do they say?

"Just give it a rub,"
says Mom.

"Go and lie down for
a while," says Dad.

"Come here and I'll kiss
it better," says Grandma.

When my Space Thruster spins out of control
and I veer into the path of a deadly asteroid
belt that leaves me bleeding and broken, what
do they say?

"Just give it a rub,"
says Mom.

"Go and lie down for
a while," says Dad.

"Come here and I'll kiss
it better," says Grandma.

10

When the vine snaps as I swing across the crocodile-infested river and I'm bumped and thumped about on the rocks below, what do they say?

"Just give it a rub,"
says Mom.

"Go and lie down for
a while," says Dad.

"Come here and I'll kiss
it better," says Grandma.

When I've been diving for sunken treasure in the Caribbean and my air tank's run out and I only just reach the surface, gulping and gasping for air, what do they say?

"Just give it a rub," says Mom.

"Go and lie down for a while," says Dad.

"Come here and I'll kiss it better," says Grandma.

Yesterday, I decided that when I grow up I'm going to be a doctor. Then every time a grownup comes to see me with the flu, or a broken leg, or an ingrown toenail, I know exactly what I'll say . . .

"Just give it a rub."

"Go and lie down for a while," or,

"Come here and I'll kiss it better!"